D0622664

The BABY SWAP

Dedicated to the memory of Jan Ormerod

1946–2013

LITTLE SIMON
An imprint of Simon & Schuster Children's Publishing Division
1230 Avenue of the Americas, New York, New York 10020

First published in 2013 Australia by Little Hare Books
First Little Simon hardcover edition February 2015

Manufactured in China through Asia Pacific Offset Ltd. 1214 HGE
2 4 6 8 10 9 7 5 3 1
Library of Congress Cataloging-in-Publication Data
Ormerod, Jan. The baby swap / by Jan Ormerod ; illustrated by Andrew Joyner. — First edition. pages cm Summary: Caroline Crocodile goes to a baby shop to see if she can exchange her drooly brother, but finds that the baby panda is a fussy eater, the baby elephant too squirty—and her brother has reason to drool. [1. Babies—Fiction. 2. Brothers and sisters—Fiction. 3. Jealousy—Fiction. 4. Crocodiles—Fiction. 5. Animals—Infancy—Fiction.] I. Joyner, Andrew, illustrator. II. Title. PZ7.O634Bab 2015
[E]—dc23 2013047673 ISBN 978-1-4814-1914-7

by Jan Ormerod • pictures by Andrew Joyner

LITTLE SIMON
New York London Toronto Sydney New Delhi

"Your baby brother is gorgeous," said Mama Crocodile.
"He is as green as a grub, and his eyes are as yellow as egg yolks."

Caroline Crocodile was jealous. "He's smelly."

The CLOCK SHOP
The Baby Shop

"He loves to eat up
his fish and frogs,"
said Mama Crocodile.

Caroline was very jealous.
"He's no fun," she said.

Mama Crocodile said, “Look at his adorable snout.”
Caroline was very, very jealous.

“He dribbles.”

"He has such scaly skin and sharp little claws," said Mama.

"He takes up all the room on your lap," said Caroline.

But Mama Crocodile was busy giving baby brother a big, smacky-smoochy kiss.

Caroline was very, very, very jealous.

She wanted a big, smacky-smoochy kiss from Mama Crocodile.

The next day Mama Crocodile said, “This new hat is not exactly what I want. I will go to the Hat Shop and swap it for one that is just right.”

“Be a good girl, Caroline, and look after your baby brother,” said Mama. “I will be back soon.”

Caroline waited, and baby brother dribbled.

Then Caroline saw that they were outside the Baby Shop, so she took him in.

"This baby brother is not exactly what I want," she said. "It's smelly and it dribbles, it's no fun, and it takes up all the room on my mama's lap. I want to swap it for one that is just right."

“Of course,” said the assistant.
“How about a baby panda? So soft and cuddly.”

“Well, my mama does love yellow eyes,”
said Caroline.

“Why don’t you try it and see?”

So Caroline Crocodile took the baby panda to the cafe for a snack.

“Fish?” asked Caroline. “Or frog?”

The baby panda ate the bamboo chair he was sitting on.
Then he ate Caroline's chair too.

Caroline took the panda back to the Baby Shop.

"No good," said Caroline.
"Fussy eater."

GOO
GA
$

"How about this baby elephant with the adorable trunk?" said the assistant.

"Well, the trunk looks like a snout, and my mama loves a snout," said Caroline.

Caroline Crocodile took the baby elephant to the fountain.

He trumpeted loudly and sprayed water over his back and onto passersby. Then he sat on the edge of the fountain and it broke.

Caroline took the elephant back to the Baby Shop.

"No good," she said.
"Too squirty."

"Well, will you try twin baby tigers?" said the assistant. "Twice the fun! And such sharp little claws."

"My mama loves sharp claws," said Caroline.

The two teeny tigers took off to the Toy Shop.

They pushed the little ones off their chairs, scattered the jigsaw puzzles, knocked over the displays, ripped up the cuddly toys, crashed the cars, and bit the books.

Caroline took the twin tigers back to the Baby Shop.

"No good," she said. "Too tiring."

"How about a baby giraffe?"
said the assistant.

"No good," said Caroline.
"My mama likes scaly babies."

"A baby pig?" the assistant suggested.

"No good," said Caroline.
"My mama likes green babies."

"Well, all I have left," said the assistant,
"is this secondhand crocodile.
It is in lovely condition:
look at its shiny new tooth."

"My baby brother, with a new tooth!
That is why he was dribbling!"
cried Caroline Crocodile. "I'll have
you back. You are still smelly and dribbly,
but you are not a fussy eater. You are
not too squirty or too tiring. . . .

You are just right after all!"

Mama Crocodile came back with her new hat.

"What a good big sister you are to look after your baby brother so well," she said. "Why, he has a new tooth! When all his teeth grow, he will be as beautiful as you are, Caroline, with your green scaly skin, your yellow eyes, your sharp little claws, and adorable snout."

FISH AND FROG

And Mama Crocodile gave Caroline a big, smacky-smoochy kiss.